SUNNY MAKES HER CASE

JENNIFER L. HOLM & MATTHEW HOLM
WITH COLOR BY LARK PIEN & GEORGE WILLIAMS

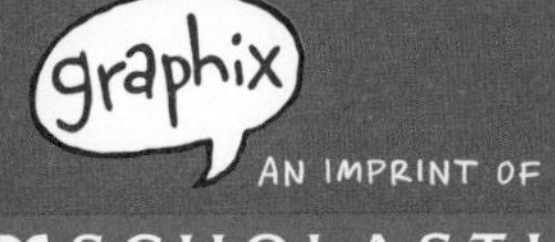

Library of Congress data available

ISBN 978-1-338-79245-4 (hardcover)
ISBN 978-1-338-79244-7 (paperback)

10 9 8 7 6 5 4 3 2 1 24 25 26 27 28

Printed in China 62
First edition, February 2024
Lettering by Fawn Lau
Colors by Lark Pien & George Williams
Edited by David Levithan
Book design by Carina Taylor
Creative Director: Phil Falco
Publisher: David Saylor

For Mr. and Mrs. Cusumano
— our favorite teachers.

CHAPTER ONE: Trophies

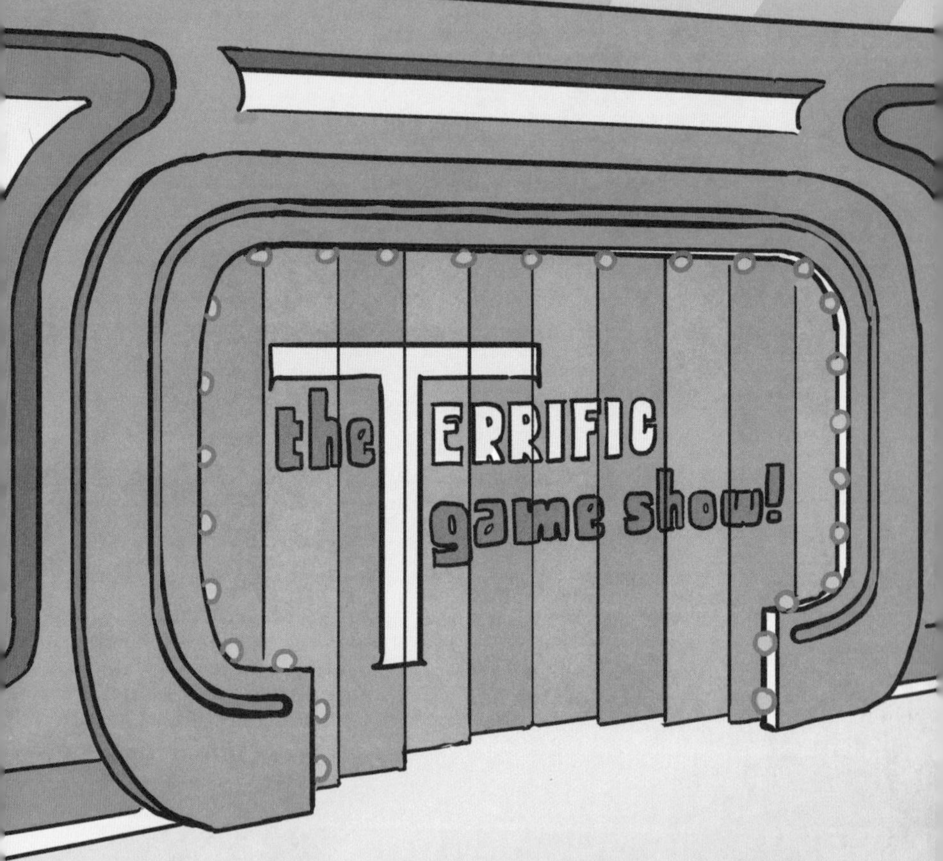

SWOOSH!

And welcome back!
We are in the final round with our two remaining contestants.

The winner of this final round will receive...
SUNNY
5070

An AM-FM radio!

A state-of-the-art toaster oven!

And a **COLOR**—yes, **COLOR**—television!
the TERRIFIC game show!

Ooooh! Color!!??!
SUNNY
5070

And, of course, the trophy!
Terrific!
5070
Woo-hoo!
Oof!
BONK!
4200
5070
LEAP!

September 1978

Ooof!

BONK!

ZOOM!

Pennsylvania

1ST PLACE
DISTRICT
CHAMPIONS
FOOTBALL
1977
1ST · BASEBALL
1976
FIELD
HOCKEY
STATE
2ND PLACE
1972
Hey, Sunny!

Tony!

Nice shirt.

GRIN!

So how are you doing?
Pretty good.

You trying out for a team?
I don't know. Maybe?
What about you?

I play ice hockey.

I've only played softball, and that was back in elementary school.

Spring 1974

Sunny!
COACH
Sunny!

Sunny!
Sunny!
H

WHIZZZZ-
Huh.
19

I, umm...

So, um, I was wondering...

Hmmm?
Uhhh?

RIIIIIIIIIIIINNG!!!

Oh no!
My class is on the top floor all the way at the end.

Better run!

ZOOP!

Sigh.

CHAPTER TWO:
Salisbury Steak

Later.
...permission slips will need to be in by Wednesday.
And tryouts for all sports teams will begin next week.

French class.
je suis
tu es
il est
elle est
ROOM 205
FRENCH

I'm going to try out for cheer!
I've been practicing my routine.
nous sommes
That's great, Deb!

Hey—why don't you try out, too?
Me?

I mean, you are pretty coordinated, right?
You already know swing flag.

TOSS
TWIRL
May 1977

We'll get to go to all the football games!

And get to wear those cute uniforms!

Maybe we'll each get to date a player!

It's so cool.

C'mon.
Pleeeeeease?

Okay, sure.

Great!
Come over to my house after school and we can practice routines.

Excusez-moi, Mademoiselle Sunny et Mademoiselle Deb?

Are you two finished talking so we may begin class?

je suis
tu es
il est
elle est

FRENCH LEVEL 1-3

Lunch.
SALISBURY STEAK
Yech.

I wonder where Deb and the girls are?

Humph.
Hiya, Sunny.

ARUN!
FRIEND!
HE'S REALLY GOOD AT D&D!
SMART COOKIE!

Want to sit together?
That'd be great.

Soon.

I just hate it so much.
Me too.
I wonder if it's even real meat.

Some kid found a bobby pin in it last year.

I heard that, too. Pretty sure it was from a lunch lady.
But that's not really the thing I hate.

Then what do you hate?
Everything!

Like that!
Huh?

1972
FOOTBALL STATE CHAMPIONS
1974
FOOTBALL STATE CHAMPIONS
1976
BASEBALL DIVISION CHAMPIONS
1972
BASKETBALL STATE CHAMPIONS
1973
BASKETBALL STATE CHAMPIONS
1975
FIELD HOCKEY DIVISION CHAMPIONS
EXIT

This whole school—everything is sports!
All anyone cares about is winning football games!
And soccer games!
And track meets!

There should be something else for us to do.
Something important.
Like a debate club.
What's that?

You debate important topics.
You know, argue.

Like whether Salisbury steak is actually made from melted tires?

It definitely is.
STATE CHAMPIONS
STATE CHAMPIONS
DIVISION CHAMPIONS
STATE CHAMPIONS
STATE CHAMPIONS
DIVISION CHAMPIONS
STATE CHAMPIONS
STATE CHAMPIONS
EXIT
HA! HA! HA! HA!

CHAPTER THREE: Tumble

Now, just do what I do to warm up, okay?

Got it!

BE
AGGRESSIVE!

BE!
BE!

AGGRESSIVE!

BE AGGRESSIVE!

BE, BE AGGRESSIVE!

Good!
This is easy!

The next day. Gym class.

Okay, start running!

SWISH

BONK!

Great catch!
HA HA
HA HA HA!

Friday.
HOME OF THE FERRETS

All right, ladies. Let's get started.

First up is Lauren Anderson.

I'm Lauren.

We incorporate a lot of tumbling into our routines
So show me a cartwheel and a back handspring.
Okay.

Sunny?
Sunny Lewin?

Let's
see your
tumbling.

Uh-oh.
WOBBLE
WOBBLE

CRASH!

Ugh!

A few days later.

I made the cut!

Me too!
Wow!!
Oh no!

CHEER SQUAD FINALISTS

Lauren Anderson	Sarah Reitman
Linda Gilbert	Deb Rogers
Sabrina Hyde	Yolanda Sanchez
Amanda Kelley	Tracy Stahl
Erin McKee	Jennifer Turner
Lisa Nardone	Nicole Williams
Donna Pitetti	Ellen Zytowski

CHAPTER FOUR: Future Lawyer

The next day.
I know Coach is going to make us run.
We get to pick up uniforms!
Practice is going to be hard today!
Do you think we'll even get to play?

A little later.

ABC
Afterschool
Specials

Oooh!

AFTERSCHOOL SPECIAL

TV SHOW AIRS AT 4:30PM

POPULAR TOPICS INCLUDE DIVORCE, DRUG ABUSE, AND ICE-SKATING!

DRAMAS THAT FEATURE "SERIOUS" ISSUES FOR KIDS AND TEENS!

USUALLY HAVE A HAPPY ENDING!

But what do I do now???

Sunny! Come help me with the groceries.

This is the last one.

Sunny, I know you didn't make the cheer team, but you need to do something after school besides watch TV.

But I just brought in the groceries.
See, I'm doing something!

Boredom and young adults are not a good combination.
But I'm not bored.

Look what happened to Dale!

DALE!
SUNNY'S OLDER BROTHER
MADE REALLY POOR CHOICES
GOT INTO LOTS OF TROUBLE
HAD TO ATTEND A BOYS' ACADEMY
BUT...NOW SERVING IN THE NAVY!

It's not fair to compare me to Dale.
I'm me! I've never gotten into trouble.
SHAKE SHAKE

SIGH
I'm sorry. You're right. But I just don't want to see you go down that path.

I won't. I promise.

And besides, Dale's straightened out.
He's doing great.

You're right, of course.
And I'M right about you having to do something after school.
Watching TV IS doing something.
That's how I learned all about "stranger danger."

You know, you're really good at arguing.
Maybe you should be a lawyer when you grow up.

Huh.

The next day.

What's up, Sunny?

Let's do it.
Do what?
Debate team.

But the school doesn't have a debate team.

Ha-ha. Wow. Are we really doing this?

It'll be easier than a backflip, trust me.

CHAPTER FIVE:
Adviser

The next day.

Hey, I heard about cheer.

You okay?

It's fine. I'm going to do debate.

Sure!

I was worried you'd feel left out with me going to cheer after school.

SHAKE SHAKE

It's okay. I'm fine.

Cool! Our first game is in two weeks. You want to come watch me cheer?
That sounds fun.
You too, Tony?
Sure!

RIIING!

After school.
Ready?
Yep.
So what do we do first?

Well, we're technically not an "official after-school club."
Huh?

We need an adviser for the team—a teacher to sponsor us.

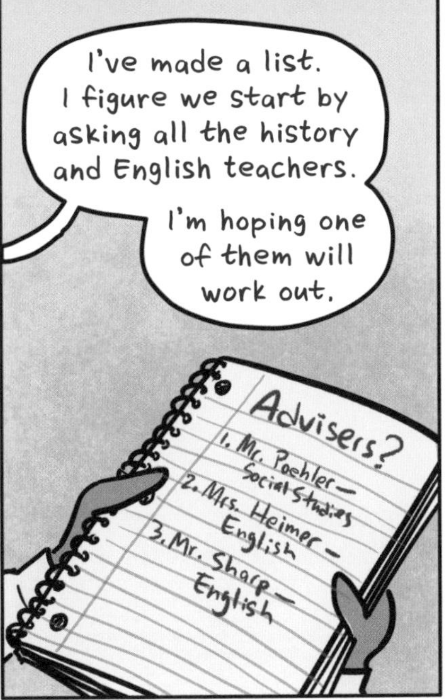
I've made a list. I figure we start by asking all the history and English teachers.
I'm hoping one of them will work out.
Advisers?
1. Mr. Poehler—Social Studies
2. Mrs. Heimer—English
3. Mr. Sharp—English

A little later.

EUROPEAN HISTORY
HOLY ROMAN EMPIRE
-Read Chapters 3-4

...which is why we wanted to ask you first!

...which is why we wanted to ask you first!

...which is why we wanted to ask you first!

...which is why we wanted to ask you first!

Well, that was a waste of time.
Do you think we should maybe ask some science teachers?
WHIIIRRRR

WHIRRRR...

CLICK!
WHIIIRRRR

What are you kids up to?
Shouldn't you be at your club?

This is it.
We're the debate team.

Really?
I always wanted to be on the debate team when I was in school.

Maybe we should ask him to be our adviser.
At least he's interested.

The next day.
For warm-up today, I'd like you to write a paragraph about something that is on your mind.

Sunny Lewin

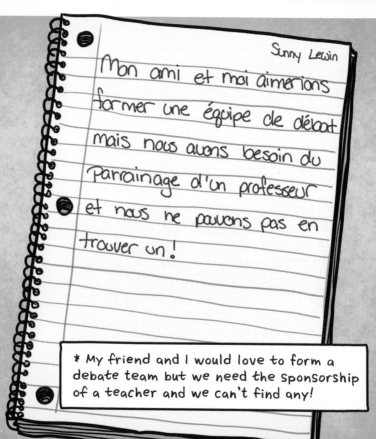

Mon ami et moi aimerions
former une équipe de débat
mais nous avons besoin du
parrainage d'un professeur
et nous ne pouvons pas en
trouver un!

* My friend and I would love to form a debate team but we need the sponsorship of a teacher and we can't find any!

Later.
RIIIINNNNNNNNGGGGGG
Good job, everyone.
Please study chapter five and work on your conjugations.

Sunny, can I speak with you for a moment?

I know someone who would be your club adviser.
You do?

NOD
My husband, Mr. Roy. The physics teacher.

Physics teachers like to debate?

My husband certainly does.
HA HA HA

After school.

...and Mrs. Roy said she thought you might be interested. She told me that you used to debate in college and that you were really good!

And you were the first—I mean, second person we thought of to be our adviser!

I'd be happy to be your debate coach.

Unless I could convince you to be on the physics team?

CHAPTER SIX: Candy

SUNNY!
BLINK!

I think you missed the bus.

7:45

Ugh.
I'll ask Gramps for a ride to school.

The bald eagle remains on the endangered species list.

Bald eagles endangered? Now that is a crying shame.

So what do you have on the agenda for today?

A French test.
Oh, and I have my first meeting of the debate team after school.
SQUEEEK!
Have a good day, old girl.
Do you need a lift home this afternoon?
That'd be great, thanks! See you at 4:30?

After school.

We're going to have our first debate today.

The two of you will be debating...

Candy!

Candy?

Yes. You are going to debate which candy is the best. And when you're done debating, we can eat it!

All right, pick a piece of candy to defend.
I'll give you ten minutes to work on your points.

Ten minutes later.

Who wants to be up first?

You can go, Sunny.
Okay.

I chose BOTTLE CAPS.

BOTTLE CAPS
the soda pop candy

First of all, they come in a lot of tasty flavors, so you have a choice.

Second, they're bottle caps! Pretty cool, right?
Most candy has boring shapes, but not Bottle Caps.

That's why Bottle Caps are the best candy.

Not bad.
Arun?

Ahem
Gobstoppers are the clearly superior candy.

It's not that they last forever—although I haven't personally timed eating one.

It's because you can't just bite into one like a lollipop.
You have to suck on it for a long time.

It teaches you patience.

Which helps build character.

This is why

Gobstoppers
are clearly

the
SUPERIOR
candy.

Later.

How did your debate go?

I should have picked the Gobstopper.

CHAPTER SEVEN:
Both Sides

The most important part of being a good debater is the ability to see both sides of an issue.
Both sides? But I thought there was only one right side.
SHAKE
SHAKE
It's the judges who will decide which side gets to be called the right one.

In a real debate, you don't even know which side you will be assigned.

So you have to be prepared to argue for either.

Affirmative / Negative
So let's practice seeing both sides of an issue.

Affirmative / Negative

The negative side argues **AGAINST** the motion.

Sunny, you will argue for the affirmative side. Arun, you will argue for the negative side.

Affirmative / Negative

MOTION: Resolved:
PB & J is a good sandwich

Here is the resolution.

I'm going to give you ten minutes to think about your argument.

Ten minutes later.

Start by greeting the audience. Then repeat the resolution in the affirmative.

Hello, audience. The resolution is: "Resolved: PB&J is a good sandwich."
I am arguing for the affirmative side.

Um, PB&J is a good sandwich because, um, it's, um, tasty.

Also, it's really easy to eat.
It's a sandwich even kids can make!

Finally, it's healthy. Peanuts are good for you.

Also, I don't think your argument is persuading me all that much. You're missing the secret sauce:

Passion!

You're up, Arun!

Affirmative / Negative
MOTION: Resolved:
PB & J is a good sandwic
Honored judges, despite my opponent's words, it's clear that PB&J is **NOT** a good sandwich.

First, there is nothing tasty about peanut butter.
It sticks to the roof of your mouth.

Second, although PB&J is easy to make, it's also easy to pour yourself a bowl of sugary cereal.
But sugary cereal isn't a healthy meal.

Finally, jelly is full of sugar. And sugar is bad for your teeth.

/Negative
In short, PB&J is **NOT** a good sandwich.
Thank you.

CLAP CLAP
CLAP
Well done, Arun!

SHAKE
SHAKE

The next morning.

Do you want a peanut butter and jelly sandwich for your lunch, Sunny?

Huh. But she's always loved PB&J.

CHAPTER EIGHT:
Game Day

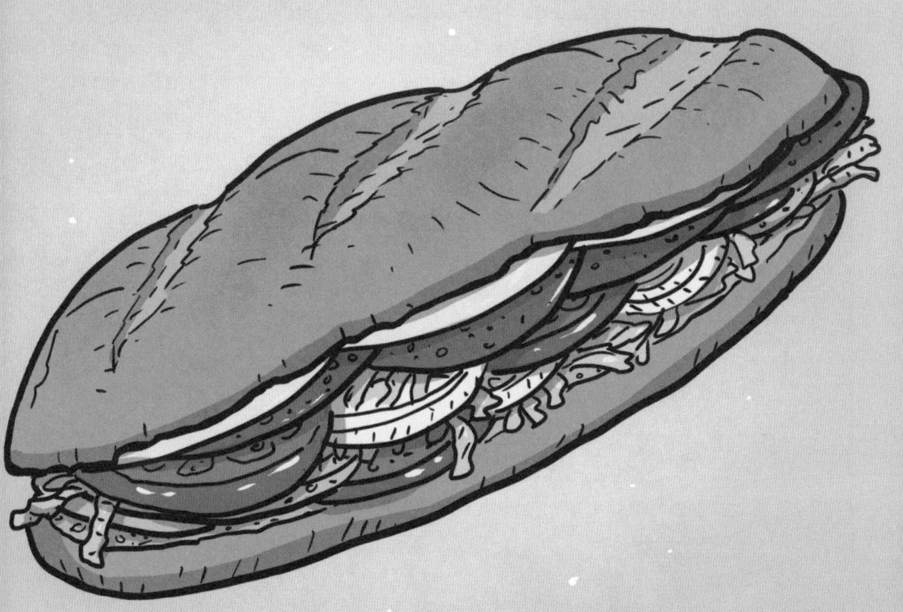

72
10
23
81

Everyone ready for Game Day on Saturday?

THE FERRETS
FERRETS! FERRETS! FIGHTING FERRETS!

Do you think they'd ever have a pep rally for a debate match?

Uh, probably not?
Exactly.
It's so unfair.

My ideal school wouldn't even have a gym.
Just a huge library.

That's it?

And maybe a room with a pinball machine and a TV. Why not?

The next day.

TAP
TAP

Hey, Sunny!
Are you going to the game on Saturday?

Yep! I promised Deb I would watch her cheer.
NOD

Great! I'll save you a seat!

Saturday.

Does Mom know you're staying for the game?

I think she's figured it out by now.

HOAGIES!

THEY'RE SOMETIMES CALLED "SUB SANDWICHES" IN OTHER PARTS OF THE COUNTRY!

HAM, PROVOLONE CHEESE, LETTUCE, TOMATOES, ONIONS, OIL, AND OREGANO!

ALWAYS TASTE BETTER THE NEXT DAY!

THE MARCHING BAND KIDS MAKE THEM AS A FUNDRAISER!

HOAGIES

I'm gonna get a hoagie. Do you want one?

Sounds good.

No, thanks. I'll find us seats.

Sunny!

Hey!

Good seats?
Great seats!

I got this for you!
You did?

I got a little bit of everything.
BIT-O-HONEY

Wow!
That was really nice.

Did I miss much of the game?
It just started.

Ooooh! Look! There's Deb!

How's debate going?
I really like it! Mr. Roy is actually kind of funny.

I bet you're great.

GULP!
Um, Sunny—
There you are, sunny!

It took me forever to find you.
Great seats!

PLUNK!

Uh, Dad, this is Tony.
Remember? From this summer?
I worked with him at the snack bar at the pool?

Of course! Great to meet you!
Want a hoagie? I got extra onions.

Um, no, thank you.

CHAPTER NINE:
Draft

After school.

I've entered our school in a local debate tournament. You two will compete as a team.
It's a good chance to get your feet wet.

LIBERTY
REGIONAL YOUTH DEBATES
Fall 1978 Schedule

A team? How does that work?

It's two-on-two.

You and Sunny will debate a team of two students from another school.

The topic is... Let's see...

Huh, the draft.

Um, I'm pretty sure the window is closed.

The military draft, when military service is not voluntary and young men are either selected by lottery or automatically obligated to go to war.

Even though it ended in 1973, it could still be reinstated if our country enters a war.

You two should start doing research now.

And you have to be prepared to argue both sides: affirmative and negative.

That weekend.

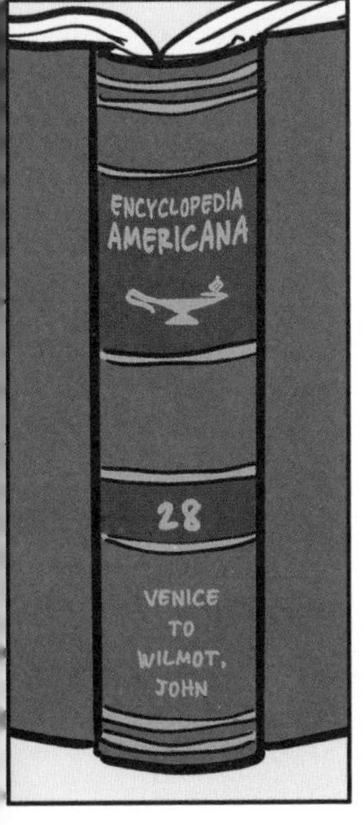
ENCYCLOPEDIA
AMERICANA
28
VENICE
TO
WILMOT,
JOHN

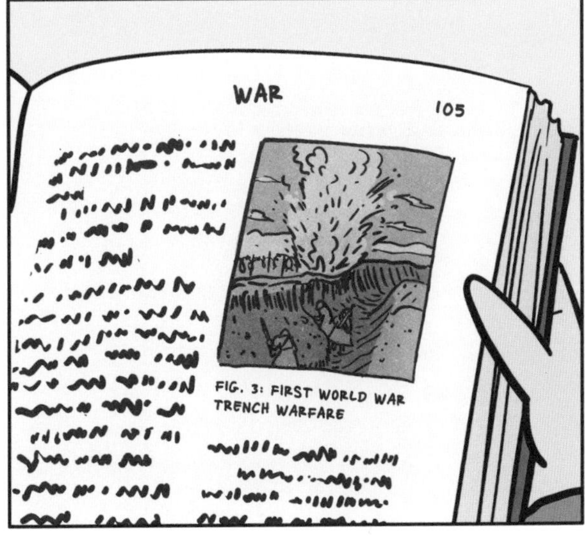
WAR
105
FIG. 3: FIRST WORLD WAR
TRENCH WARFARE

FIG. 4: D-DAY LANDING AT OMAHA BEACH, NORMANDY, FRANCE, DURING THE SECOND WORLD WAR.

FIG. 5: RAISING THE FLAG ON MOUNT SURIBACHI, IWO JIMA, PACIFIC THEATER, WORLD WAR TWO

Why the big sigh, old girl?

The motion is: "Resolved: The draft is a necessary tool." We have to be able to argue both sides.

The problem is that I don't have **ANY** affirmative arguments!
Look!

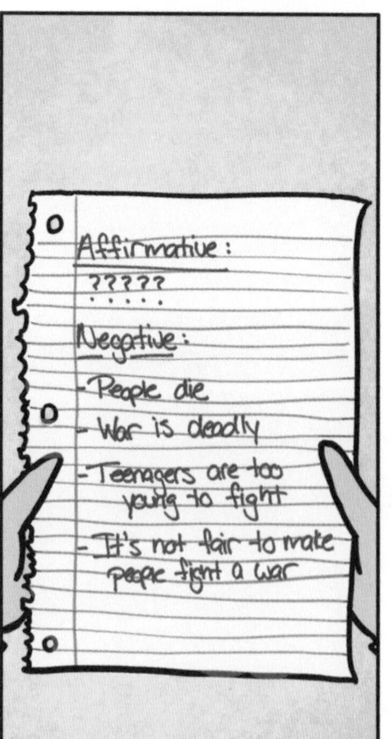
Affirmative:
?????
Negative:
- People die
- War is deadly
- Teenagers are too young to fight
- It's not fair to make people fight a war

You were in World War II, right?
So what do you think about the draft?
My brother and I were both drafted into the army.

It's a terrible thing.

I know!
What's good about being sent to war as a teenager?
You could die!

But sometimes you have to make sacrifices. I don't think we would have won World War II without the draft.
We simply didn't have enough soldiers to fight the Germans and the Japanese on two sides.

And if we'd lost!

Everyone we loved—all of our families and friends—could have died.

But I'm an old man.

The next day.
Dad, is it okay if I call Dale?

You want to call JAPAN????

It's for a school project.

Okay. But keep it short. We're not millionaires.

1970S LONG-DISTANCE CALLS

THE OLDEN DAYS!
CALLS OUT OF STATE (OR OUT OF COUNTRY) WERE SUPER-EXPENSIVE
THERE WERE NO CELL PHONES

Hi, may I speak to Dale Lewin?
Hang on— let me find him.

It's Sunny!
Sunny! Is everything okay?
LEWIN
Yeah. I just wanted to talk.
How's Japan?
It's neat. The food is different.
I ate raw fish.
LEWIN
Yuck!

So I have a question. Were you drafted into the navy?

Nope, I enlisted. The draft is just for during war.

LEWIN

Do you think they kiss?

Ugh, I hope not...

CHAPTER TEN:
Treats
LIFESAVERS
Reese's
CUPS
SNICKERS
SNICKERS

Dad is going away for a work trip on Halloween.

Do you want to stay home and give out candy or take Teddy trick-or-treating?

Summy?

Fine, I'll take him, and you can give out candy.
SHAKE
SHAKE

Thanks, honey.

The next day.
So how'd you do on the quiz?
I studied really hard.
I can't believe I didn't do better.
Maybe ask if you can do some extra-credit work?
Good idea.
By the way, what are you doing for Halloween?
I have to take my little brother trick-or-treating.

Maybe later we can go to the snack bar and try to deep-fry some of the candy we get.

HA!

Halloween night.

Trick or tweet!
DING-DONG!

Aren't you a sweet bear?
ROOOOAAARRR!!!

Thank you!
No more roaring, Teddy!

Sorry I'm late!

Hey, Tony! Nice costume.
Well, I kind of had it lying around already.

And you must be Teddy.
No, I'm a fiewce bear!
ROOOAAARRRR!!!

Are you supposed to be a... businessman?
I object!

Huh?

I'm a lawyer, silly.

ROAARR!
ROARR!!
He's really good at roaring.
A little **TOO** good if you ask me.

So how's ice hockey going?
15

Great!
I'm going to be starting this year.

How long have you been playing?
Since I was five.

Five??!

Yeah. My dad kind of wants his own hockey team.
As soon as we could skate, he put a stick in our hands.

So, is it annoying having to play ice hockey?

Definitely not! I **LOVE** ice hockey!

In school, I get B's and C's and I have to work hard for all of them.
But out there on the ice, I know I'm good at something.

I get it.
NOD

ROAR ROAR
ROOOAARRR!!!!

You can't have my candy!
SHAKE
I'M A HUNGRY BEAR!!

Well, I'm a hungry witch.
I'll turn you into a rat.

We better go rescue Teddy before she goes through with it.
ROOOAAARR!
Zap! You're a rat!
15

CHAPTER ELEVEN:
Debate

LIBERTY
DEBATES
TODAY

SCHOOL SIGN-IN

We haven't had your school compete before.
We're a new team.
How nice.

CAFETORIUM

ARDMORE

DEBATE BASICS

"LINCOLN-DOUGLAS-STYLE DEBATE"

JUDGES CHOOSE WINNER BUT ALSO GIVE A SCORE.

THE SPEAKERS ARE TIMED.

BOTH SIDES "REBUT" THE OTHER SIDES' ARGUMENTS.

SHAKE HANDS AT THE END.

All right, debaters. Here is our topic:

"Resolved: that the federal government should institute the draft of eligible men during wartime."

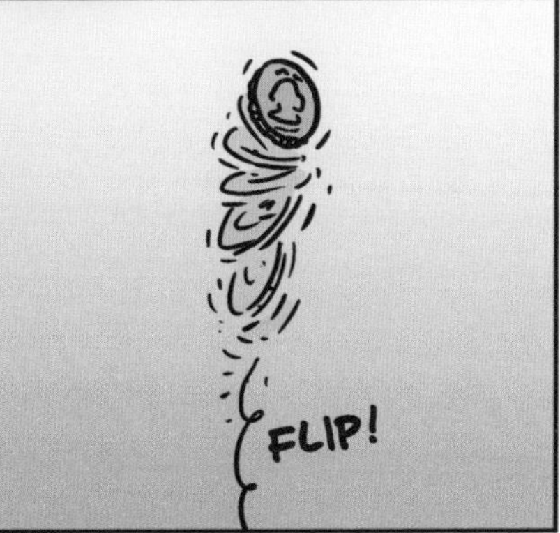

Later.

Good debate, students.

Both teams were very impressive.

That afternoon.

And the two schools that will debate the final round are...

St. Malachi's and Fairview.

Uh, how did we get here?

I don't know, but whatever we did, let's keep doing it.

Later.

...which is why the draft is simply wrong. It is unfair to force people to fight and possibly die.

For the final rebuttal for the affirmative: Sunny Lewin.

GULP!

I have two brothers, and I wouldn't want them to be drafted.

And if I were a boy, I wouldn't want to get drafted.

Nobody wants to die!

But sometimes it's not about you.

What if your family—your mom and dad and little brother—would die if someone didn't protect them?

Would you fight then?

The draft is a terrible sacrifice.
And sometimes it's the only hope we have to protect everything— and everyone— we love.

Thank you.

2ND PLACE

Say "cheese!"

FLASH!

2ND PLACE

CHAPTER TWELVE: Spontaneous Debate

The football team continued their streak with another win on Saturday!
Let's hear it for our Fighting Ferrets!

The marching band will be selling hoagies at lunch.

Finally, the debate team took second place on Saturday in a local competition.
Have a great day!

We have a debate team?
News to me.

After school.

Ready to go?
We have a tournament to prepare for.

We do?
Huh?

Because you placed in the debate, you're eligible to compete in the regional tournament in a few weeks!

Is it going to be on the draft again?

It's a spontaneous debate.
LIBERTY

Does that mean it could happen any time?
Is it happening right now?

No, it means the debate topic will be announced at the debate itself.
So you don't have to do any specific research.
CHUCKLE

Only the best debaters succeed in a spontaneous debate.

But what if it's a topic we don't know anything about?
Exactly! I like to be prepared! I **LIKE** index cards!

Um, is this the debate team?

I heard you guys started a debate team!
Where's everybody else?

Um, it's just us.
So far.

I can't believe you guys took first place in that tournament! That's amazing!

Actually, it was second place.
But thanks.
So can I? Join, I mean?

Uh, sure.
Sure.

Great!
By the way, I'm Jason!
Arun.
Sunny.

Welcome to the team, Jason.

Looks like you've officially arrived.

CHAPTER THIRTEEN: Ties

SALE

What are we shopping for?
I need a new tie. I'm taking Myrtle out for her birthday.

They look so uncomfortable.

Ties are important.
When you wear a tie, people take you seriously.

A little later.
HOWARD JOHNSON'S
I love HoJo's.
Me too.

HOWARD JOHNSON'S!

Here ya go. Two clam strip rolls, one ginger ale, and a Sanka.

Thanks!

Looks delicious!

Did you play sports when you were in school?
I played baseball.

Were you any good?

Yep! It was the best thing I ever did.
NOD

Why?
It taught me how to lose.
Why would you need to learn how to lose?

Because it's important.
When you lose, it makes you think about what you can do better next time.
So you work harder and come up with new ideas. It makes you hungry.

So, losing is better than winning?
No, winning is much better.
Nobody wants to lose.

EYE ROLL

CHAPTER FOURTEEN:
Mock

We're going to do mock debates for the next week.
MOCK DEBATES

What's that?
It's a practice debate!

Exactly. Since we don't know what topic you will end up debating, you need to get used to thinking on your feet.

I've put a bunch of topics in this bowl.

Now, these topics will not be easy. You will probably not even agree with the side you have to argue for.

Arguing for an issue you don't agree with forces you to see that issue from the other side.

You're not going to meet too many people in life who agree with you on everything. So learning to understand where someone is coming from is a crucial life skill. It will make you a great debater and an even better human being.

You and Sunny will debate this.

Arun, I want you to judge them.

Let's flip a coin and pick sides.

I won! I'll take the affirmative!
Negative, I guess.
PING!
Affirmative is up first.

MOCK DEBATES

It should be clear that animals ought not to be kept in zoos.

Animals are living creatures.

They are affectionate.

They have families.

The cute elephant you saw in the zoo? That elephant probably has a family back in Africa that it was stolen from.
Or the funny penguin? Can you imagine what it's like to be kidnapped from an ice floe?

Furthermore, who are we as humans—another kind of animal, really—to sentence other living things to a life in prison simply because we want to look at them? It's cruel and inhumane.

MOCK DEBATES

It's hard to argue in the face of all that emotion.

Which is why you need to take **YOUR** emotional reaction out of it.

Deep breath.

There must be **SOME** goo reasons tha zoos exist, right?

While what my opponent said is very persuasive, he's missing an important point: Zoos keep animals safe—like the bald eagle!

Zoos take care of endangered animals.

These animals have families and continue to grow. They're safe.

But if we get rid of zoos, these animals will become extinct!

OCK
EBATES
Well, Arun?
PERIODIC TABLE OF THE ELEMENTS

They were both good. Really.
Sunny's endangered species point was great.

But it's hard to beat stealing defenseless elephants and penguins.
SHRUG

YAY!
Typical.

CHAPTER FIFTEEN:
Fondue Party

Sunny, your dad and I are throwing a fondue party on Saturday night.

We need you to help out.

FONDUE PARTY!

THE HOST SERVES MELTED CHEESE IN A POT!

DIP BREAD AND MEAT INTO THE CHEESE!

SOMETIMES THERE IS MELTE CHOCOLATE AND MARSHMALLOWS

The next day.
Hey!
Hey back.

Congrats on the debate win! That's so cool!

Thanks! But the next one's going to be even harder.

Uh, yeah. Exactly.
...

So I was, um, wondering if you were busy Saturday night?

Nope!
Great! Maybe we—
Oh, wait. I forgot.
I have a fondue party.
You're going to a fondue party?
My parents are having a grown-up fondue party and my mom wants me to hand out appetizers and clean up.

RIIIINNGG!!!!
Gotcha.

See ya later.

Saturday night.
Thank you, Sunny.

These are pretty good.
They're my favorite.

How's cheer going?
Better.

Better?
I was really nervous for a bit there.

I'm one of the shortest girls on the squad.
And doing the pyramid is scary!
It looked scary to me, too!

But after practicing with the other girls, I wasn't as scared.
I knew they had my back and would catch me.
Now I feel like I can try anything!

Even a backflip?
Definitely a backflip!

Hey, maybe I can get some of the girls and we can cheer for you at your debate?
That would be great! HA!

So how's **TONY**?
Good.
Has he asked you on a date yet?
No!
So I was wondering if you were busy Saturday night?
Uh-oh.
What?
He asked me what I was doing tonight.

That was him asking you on a date, silly!

But he didn't say that! He didn't ask me out on a date! I think he would actually ask me, you know?

Then what should I do?

Nothing.

Really?

Really.

I think I liked it better when we were little and the boys just ate dirt to make us laugh.

HA HA!

CHAPTER SIXTEEN:
Pantsuit

I think he's innocent.
He's guilty.
Pretty sure the ex-wife did it.
ROAR!

VOGUE
CITY DRESSING. BASIC AND VERY, VERY SMART
Can I get a new outfit to wear to the debate tournament?
I don't see why not.

Later.

GIMBELS

GIMBELS

This outfit is cute!

The pleated skirt is adorable.

I don't want to look adorable. I want to look serious. Like a lawyer.

It's a debate tournament!

NEW!

You might want to check out the petites section in Women's.

I think they'll have what you're looking for.

Career Looks
PETITES
Ooo!
DRESSING ROOMS
Let's see, honey!

Lovely!

I think I need a tie.
A tie?
No one will take me seriously unless I'm wearing a tie.

I have just the thing.

Can I get my own briefcase?

SIGH.

CHAPTER SEVENTEEN: Negative

COMMUNITY CO
ACADEMIC HA
Good luck!
Thanks!
DEBATES
TODAY

There she is!

We have about ten minutes until the first round.
So now's a good time to use the restroom.

There they go.
I don't know why we even bother.
They're just gonna win.

Who are they?
Devon Country Day School. Fancy private boys' school.
They've won the last three years in a row.

A little later.

As you know, we are doing spontaneous topics today.
The two winners of this morning's session will go on to debate this afternoon.
All right, the topic for this first session is...

"Resolved: It is inhumane to keep animals in zoos."

HA! What are the chances?

You may begin.

This round goes
to Fairview!

That afternoon.

And the finalists for the last round, based on cumulative score, are Devon Country Day and—

And now for the topic...

"Resolved: It is better to be successful in academics than in sports."

FLIP!

Please, please, please...

Heads!

We choose affirmative.
EXIT

WINCE

Ugh. This really can't be happening.

A few minutes later.

Sunny! Pssst!

While I appreciate your enthusiasm, there will be no cheering during the debate.

All right, let's get started...

In fact, if the amount of time and effort that we focus on sports was given to academics, we would have already sent a manned rocket to Mars!

SAG

Later.
Arguing for the negative...

Fairview High.

Honored guests...

Honored guests—
GULP!

KA-THUNK!

NOD

Sure, it's easy to say that academics are more important than sports, especially when we're all up here doing something academic.

But that doesn't mean that sports aren't important.

Because sports help you to be good at life!

Later.

Finally, sports give you confidence.
If you're successful in a sport, you'll feel good about yourself.
And really, isn't that one of the most important lessons to learn?
After all, you can look up the square root of pi in an encyclopedia, but you can't look up how to feel good about yourself.

Woo!

Thank you.

CHAPTER EIGHTEEN:
Afterschool Special

Here are some more pancakes.
I still can't believe we won! It's amazing!
I knew you'd win against those silly boys, old girl!
Thanks, Gramps!

And guess what? Mr. Roy is going to throw us a pizza party after school!

We're just so proud of you, Sunny.
Your dad suggested we take you out for a celebratory dinner this week. Sound good?

Sure!
ROAAARRR!!!

I'm not sure if we should invite any bears to dinner.
HA HA
HA HA HA HA HA HA
HA HA

Later.
The field hockey team has taken second place in the district championships.
Let's hear it for our Fighting Ferrets!

The marching band will be selling hoagies at lunch today.
YAWN

And the debate team took first place in a debate tournament this past weekend.

We have a debate team?
Since when?

After school
Pizza's here!

Thanks.
For what?
For starting the debate team with me!

You sound like an afterschool special.
Well, it is after school, right?
Get it?
GUFFAW!

Students, this is Ms. Siegel from the local paper.

I'm doing a story on your debate team win.

So tell me, whose idea was it to start the debate team?

Well, it was Sunny's idea.

It was Arun's idea.

The next day.

Local Happenings

The Bulletin 21

First-Time Debate Team Sweeps First-Place Honors

Fairview team members (L to R) Arun Patel, Sunshine Lewin, and Jason Phillips won Saturday's Liberty Debates

Pa. Polka bands sign for festival

Sale! 20%

Our name means...

We didn't get a pep rally, but this is pretty cool!
I can't believe my eyes are shut.

Hey, Sunny!
Hi!
See you tomorrow, Sunny.

Really?
That would be great!

If you can watch me debate, I can watch you skate.

Maybe after the game we can go out and get something to eat.

You know, like a date.

GULP

Sure.
That sounds good.

Where should we go?
How about HoJo's?
I love their milkshakes.

Me too.

A NOTE FROM JENNIFER L. HOLM & MATTHEW HOLM

Sunny's debating experience was inspired by Jenni's own life. She and her friend, Kaustuv Banjeree, started the debate club at their high school. They were fortunate to have an incredible English teacher, Mr. Cusumano, act as their debate coach. Despite the odds, this brand-new team managed to take second place in a regional debate competition. Everyone was surprised, especially Jenni and Kaustuv!

JENNIFER L. HOLM & MATTHEW HOLM are the award-winning brother-sister team behind the Babymouse and Squish series. Jennifer is also the author of many acclaimed novels, including three Newbery Honor books and the NEW YORK TIMES bestseller THE FOURTEENTH GOLDFISH.

LARK PIEN is an indie cartoonist from Oakland, California. She has published many comics and is the colorist for Printz Award winner AMERICAN BORN CHINESE and BOXERS & SAINTS. Her characters Long Tail Kitty and Mr. Elephanter have been adapted into children's books. You can follow her on Twitter @larkpien.

GEORGE WILLIAMS is a comic artist and colorist from the UK. He is the co-creator and illustrator of LET ME OUT (Oni Press), as well as the illustrator of the graphic novel CROC N' ROLL with Hamish Steele. He can be found on twitter @neatodon.